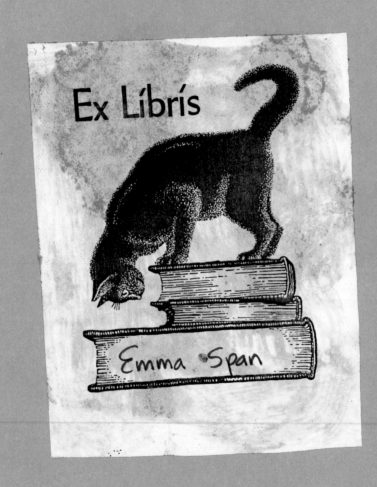

Ex Libris

Emma Span

Mrs. Huggins and Her Hen Hannah

LYDIA DABCOVICH

E. P. DUTTON NEW YORK

in memory of Norma Farber,
who gave Mrs. Huggins her name

Library of Congress Cataloging in Publication Data
Dabcovich, Lydia.   Mrs. Huggins and her hen Hannah.
Summary: Mrs. Huggins' contented relationship with
her hen Hannah comes to an unfortunate end but is reborn
in an unexpected way.
1. Children's stories, American.   [1. Chickens—
Fiction.   2. Death—Fiction]   I. Title.
PZ7.D12Mr   1985   [E]   85-4406
ISBN 0-525-44203-0

Published in the United States by E. P. Dutton,
2 Park Avenue, New York, N.Y. 10016

Published simultaneously in Canada by
Fitzhenry & Whiteside Limited, Toronto

Editor: Ann Durell   Designer: Edith T. Weinberg

Printed in Hong Kong by South China Printing Co.
First Edition   W   10 9 8 7 6 5 4 3 2 1

Mrs. Huggins lived with her hen Hannah.
Together they did everything.

They cooked and baked

and cleaned and scrubbed.

They did the wash

and hung it up to dry.

Together they planted,
raked and watered their garden,

and picked ripe apples and red tomatoes
for tasty pies and juicy stews.

Together they sheared the sheep

and milked the cow.

Every evening, by their warm fire,
they stitched and darned.

Then they yawned and stretched,
wound the clock, said good-night
and went to bed.

One day, Hannah got sick.

Mrs. Huggins nursed her day and night.

But very soon, Hannah died.
Mrs. Huggins was very sad.
She buried Hannah in a green meadow.

The cottage seemed very empty without
Hannah. Mrs. Huggins sat and cried.

Suddenly she heard a sound
from Hannah's nest.

And there was a fuzzy little chick.

Now Mrs. Huggins lives with
Hannah's daughter.

Together they do everything.